Valeria Ann Lomas

PRINCE ARGENT: THE SILVER PRINCE

Limited Special Edition. No. 11 of 25 Paperbacks

Valeria came from a family of four children; she was the third child.

She learned to ride at the age of eleven.

She would muck out, sweep, clean tack, groom, anything to be near the horses. She was always there, waiting to help turn the horses out into their paddocks.

Valeria moved to Dorset with her family in 1962. The first thing to find was the local stables, just a short bike ride away.

Every day after school and all weekends were spent at the stables. Later Val met Tony at the stables. He stood there smiling across the back of her favourite horse, Rani.

They married young, Val was seventeen and Tony was twenty-two, they are still married fifty-three years later.

Val worked for a vet, and as a shepherdess, but it was horses again that were the guiding force.

In 1976, they took over the stables at Etchinghill in Kent Teaching, training students for their B.H.S. exams, breaking and schooling horses. Lots of competitions, eventing and later, riding.

It was at Ridgehill that they were introduced to American Morgan horses, and they became the love of her life.

First was the beautiful Silkie (Eaglehead Silken Touch). Silkie was the inspiration for the pink and silver unicorn mare who appears in another story.

Val's dear friends Nan and Tony Philips gave her their Morgan Gelding 'Mosaic'; he was the inspiration for Prince Argent.

He was handsome, gentle, lively and gave Val so much fun. How she loved to ride him!

Now Val has two Labradors, Ruby and Indie, she and Tony enjoy walking with them in the beautiful Dorset countryside.

This book is dedicated to our Niece, Sarah Nickless.

I have written many stories for Sarah and Peter's daughters, Polly and Matilda.

It was Sarah's enthusiasm for Prince Argent that encouraged me to go to print.

With much love from your Auntie Val xx

Valeria Ann Lomas

PRINCE ARGENT: THE SILVER PRINCE

AUSTIN MACAULEY PUBLISHERS™

LONDON • CAMBRIDGE • NEW YORK • SHARJAH

A CIP catalogue record for this title is available from the British Library.

ISBN 9781528933827 (Paperback)
ISBN 9781528967624 (ePub e-book)

www.austinmacauley.com

First Published (2019)
Austin Macauley Publishers Ltd
25 Canada Square
Canary Wharf
London
E14 5LQ

I would like to thank my dear friend, Susan Homer, for her amazing support, for her humour and for listening to all of my ideas for my stories.

To my dear little sister, Jan Morris, for her help with computers, editing and all of the things that I find difficult and she finds so easy.

Finally, I'd like to thank my husband, Tony, for his support, for listening to my ideas and for his unending enthusiasm for my stories.

Chapter 1
Matilda's Birthday Wish

Prince Argent was born in Cambridgeshire, near Ely. His dam, that means his mother in horsey terms, was a Welsh mountain pony and her name was Diva. She was grey, almost white, with a long silky mane and tail.

It is not widely known that unicorns can start life as Welsh mountain ponies, but you just have to look at a quality grey Welsh pony to see the possibilities!

Matilda's mummy and daddy asked her what she would like for her seventh birthday. She put her hands behind her back, crossed her fingers and answered, "I'd like a pony please." She knew that it was a big ask!

There was a stunned silence! "We weren't expecting anything like that," said Daddy, looking a bit pale.

"Are you sure?" asked Mummy, "it means a lot of work and a huge commitment from you. Are you really sure that you're ready for that?"

"Oh, yes," said Matilda, "I've worked out exactly where she can have her stable. It's in the barn, next to the old feed room. There's a space there, that will be just right."

Her older sister, Polly, said, "Where *SHE* can have *HER* stable! So, you've already found your pony then?"

Matilda blushed and said, "Well, yes. Her name is Diva and she belongs to my friend, Jess."

So they all went over to the barn. Polly said, "I can see exactly what you mean, it's perfect! You already have two walls so, all that's needed is a side wall, the front and the door."

Daddy was warming to the idea and got out his tape measure. He started writing down measurements on his pad. Mummy smiled; it was high fives all round.

The next weekend, they all went to the local stables. There, they saw Diva: a beautiful, grey Welsh mountain pony. In the horsey world, to call a pony 'grey' means, it can be from almost black to dark grey, through to dapple grey to almost white.

Matilda's friend, Jess, was there to show Diva off. She started to explain why she had to find a new home for Diva but it was easy to see why. Just one look at her, standing next to the pony, showed you that she had simply outgrown her.

Jess mounted up and her feet were showing below Diva's belly both sides. Worst of all, her feet were knocking the jump poles down. It was time to admit that she had to find a new home for Diva.

Having to part with your beloved pony is heart-breaking, but what could be better than giving Diva into the care of her best friend, Matilda.

It was important to Jess that Diva should have a loving owner, but it was also important for her to have a nice place to live and Little Bagwood Farm, where the Nicholls family lived, was just the right place.

Mr Joyce, the farm's handy man, had just finished the stables. He had even installed automatic drinkers. There had to be two stables, because no one likes to keep a pony on its own, so Polly adopted a donkey called Poppy.

Diva and Poppy would be company for each other, as well as the lambs, chickens, bantams, two Llamas and a few ducks. The animals belonged to Sarah, Matilda's mummy.

Sarah tried so hard to train the llamas to wear their head collars and to lead them around the paddock. Polly helped with this, as she was much taller than Matilda, they were progressing quite well, but llamas could be so stubborn. Training them, to have their feet picked out, was not the easiest job on the farm. They were both a bit naughty, but not at all nasty.

Chapter 2
Diva Comes to Bagwood Farm

Matilda's birthday arrived, she was so excited because her daddy had gone to collect Diva. Daddy came into the yard, driving the Land Rover and trailer. He stopped by the barn and let down the ramp slowly, then he went into the trailer to untie Diva. He carefully turned her to let her see her new home.

Diva stood on the top of the ramp and looked at her new surroundings. She took a deep breath and called in a very loud voice. Poppy answered her and they were best friends from that moment on. Matilda took the lead rope from Daddy and led Diva into the barn, to meet her new friend and to see her new home.

Mr Joyce had whitewashed the walls of the stables and put a nice bed of wood shavings down; they looked so good. Matilda led Diva in, took off the head collar and then slipped quietly out of the door.

Diva rolled and rolled, she was covered with shavings. Then she stood up, shook the shavings out of her coat and then she blew down her nose, making everyone laugh. They gave Diva a hay net and left her and Poppy together for a couple of hours, to let them settle in.

A little later, Polly took Poppy and Matilda took Diva out to their paddock. They turned them towards the closed gate, removed their head collars and gave them treat.

Diva and Poppy turned away and trotted around the paddock, checking their new environment. Where is the water trough? Very important. Having found that, they began to graze, close together, it was very sweet.

Suddenly, Diva raised her head and her tail and did a high-stepping trot over towards the llamas, who were in the next paddock. She had never seen a llama before and was not quite sure what they were.

Not a pony and certainly not a sheep! They were like a cross between the two with a long neck, long legs and a large curly fringe, nearly covering huge, dark, beautiful eyes.

They carried their ears back and this made Diva wary of them, because when a pony or a llama lays its ears back, it means it's getting very grumpy.

They sniffed each other and made friends. Diva relaxed and soon, they were playing trotting games along the fence, between their paddocks. Poppy joined in, but half-heartedly, she thought it was a waste of energy, typical donkey!

The Pony Club were having a gymkhana at the local stables next month. Matilda was very excited and decided to take Diva.

They were getting along really well and had started jumping, with help from Mummy, who was good at designing jumping courses. They practised after school and did simple dressage, as it's so important to get the basics right.

They practised gymkhana games with help from Polly, but riding was not her favourite thing. She was a dancer and loved ballet, it was her dream to enter the Dame Darcy Bussell Dancing Academy.

The day arrived and the gymkhana was great fun. They did the clear round jumping course, and of course, got a clear round! They came second in the novice show-jumping too. Matilda was delighted and Diva seemed to carry her head just a little higher, she loved to show off.

The gymkhana games were very energetic and there were a lot of different categories. Matilda and Diva did very well and came home with lots of red rosettes – first prizes.

They had so much fun that summer, hacking out with friends. Diva's previous owner, Jess, had a new pony; he was a 14.2hh gelding, called Barney. He and Diva became great friends.

Daddy took them to the beach in Norfolk, where they stayed overnight at a friend's farm and had such fun. There were Diva, Barney and two more ponies that belonged to Jess' cousins, they loaned Mummy a lovely cob, so that she could enjoy cantering in the salty spray.

They all got soaked, but it was summer and it was warm and they all loved it. When they got back to the yard, they hosed the salt water off their ponies and cleaned the tack, using heaps of saddle soap for suppleness, to make sure that it didn't dry stiff and become uncomfortable. Then, having first cared for their ponies and tack, it was time for them to shower too.

When they were all showered, they came down for the barbeque that the daddies were cooking; it was fab. The ponies were grazing contentedly; it was the perfect end to a perfect day.

Chapter 3
The Prince

The summer seemed to whizz by. They were out every weekend at a show or an event and had a great time. One August afternoon, Matilda asked her mummy if she thought that Diva was too fat. Mummy said, "No, but we can limit her grazing, if you're worried."

"It's not that," replied Matilda. "I'm worried because when I washed her udder this morning, she squealed. I do it every day, she's never done that before and her udder is a bit fat."

Mummy said, "We've had Diva for ten and a half months and there were no stallions at the stable, so don't worry too much, I don't think that she can be in foal!"

Matilda woke early next morning. It was late August; the sun was just rising and something deep inside was telling her to hurry.

She shot into the bathroom, brushed her teeth, splashed her face, threw on her jeans and a t-shirt, ran downstairs, put on her wellies, not even socks, hopping along to get the left one on, she ran down to Diva's paddock.

There, lying in the grass near Diva, was the most beautiful foal she had ever seen!

He was grey like his mother, very unusual for a foal. When he saw Matilda, he threw up his head and leapt to his feet. He came cantering towards her on wobbly legs, calling and calling.

She ran to him and threw her arms around his neck, she closed her eyes and it felt as though they were flying! They were going over the lake, over the standing stone circle, looking down; it was just amazing!

She felt as light as a feather, as though they were a leaf in the wind, it was just awesome! That was just the first time that they would fly together.

Matilda found that she could understand, what he was thinking and he could understand, what she was thinking.

He told her that unicorns always know their partner on sight, he said that his name was Prince Argent. It means 'Silver Prince', for he was a prince amongst unicorns and ponies.

He told Matilda to put her hand on his forehead. She could feel a small bump and a vibration coming from the bump.

He said that his horn would grow there and it had started already, but only she and Diva would be able to see it. To everyone else, he would just be a very long-legged Welsh mountain pony.

Sadly, Matilda wouldn't be able to register him, because no one knew who his sire was. Sire, in horsey terms, means Father.

Diva was so proud of her stunning foal. She remembered the evening last September, when she saw a large shadow flying over the paddock. As she turned to look, to her amazement, there stood the most handsome unicorn!

Not just a unicorn, but a winged unicorn, which was so rare, and he was here for her.

He came over to her and gently nuzzled her neck. Diva was still in shock and squealed at him! He jumped back and bowed very low. He didn't want to upset her.

He folded his golden tipped wings over his back, carefully. He had been watching her for ages. Her beauty had captured his heart and now was their time.

He blinked his huge dark eyes and came a little closer. His spiralled horn was golden, as were his mane, tail and his cloven hooves. In the evening sunlight, he was just awesome!

This time she nuzzled his neck and that was her acceptance. He stayed with her for a few weeks, but then he had to go.

Oh! How she longed to see him again. She sighed, at least she had his son, and what a magnificent foal he was! He had his sire's beautiful eyes that had won over her heart.

Matilda's family all came to see the foal, they were amazed, but Mummy said, "You knew Matilda, you knew!"

"I knew something wonderful was about to happen, but wasn't sure exactly what," Matilda replied. "This is the best day of my life!" She could not explain exactly how she felt to her family, but she knew that she had a spiritual connection with Prince, and it was just awesome!

Prince grew much faster than the average foal. Unicorns are magical creatures and within a year, he had grown and matured.

Matilda still enjoyed riding Diva, but had started riding Prince in the paddock. Because they could communicate, it was so easy, and she felt part of him.

Chapter 4
A Message from the King

Time passes so quickly; Matilda was now nine years old. She had grown tall for her age. Her blonde hair was long, thick and shiny.

She had noticed many changes in Prince. He was taller, stronger and very fit for such a youngster. We must remember that he was a magical creature and therefore, was able to do things that other ponies could not do.

Matilda had outgrown Diva but she just couldn't bear to part with her, so her cousin, Abby, had Diva on loan. Abby kept Diva at lower Bagwood Farm, with her friend, Poppy, the donkey; happiness all round. They often went out riding with Matilda and Prince.

How Diva loved to watch her wonderful son. She was thrilled that only she, Prince and Matilda knew, that one day he would be ready to become a full unicorn.

The days were long, it was close to the summer solstice, the longest day, often called midsummer's day. On this day, wonderful and magical things can happen!

Matilda and Prince rode out together, just the two of them. He was restless and he wanted to keep on the move so they went to the forest. It's always cooler there. The wide rides have a cool breeze and the leaves cast a shade of dappled sunlight, so it's darker under the trees.

A silver light appeared in the shade ahead of them. It grew brighter as they approached and a beautiful creature appeared.

She had long curly auburn hair, alabaster skin and azure blue eyes. Her gown was silver and long enough to hide her feet. She hovered on silver wings that were moving so fast, it was hard to see them.

Her name was Princess Kessia. She was a woodland fairy. "Le Roi D'Ore", The Golden King, Prince's sire, had sent her with a message for Prince and Matilda.

Kessia told Matilda to ride Prince to the Henge, the ancient stone circle, on midsummer's day. At midday, they must go into the centre of the Henge together, then the magic would begin!

This exciting news was just what they had been waiting for. Princess Kessia came closer. Her beautiful blue eyes shone and she had an exotic Egyptian look.

She smiled and touched Prince on his forehead, where his horn would be. He felt the tingle as she touched him, Matilda felt it too.

They watched as Kessia ascended up to the tree canopy. As she left, the silver light went with her.

Matilda said, "We must go home to prepare for the big day, let's go as fast as the wind." So, Prince summoned up his magical powers, Matilda had to catch her breath because Prince's feet hardly touched the ground as he sped homeward.

Chapter 5
Metamorphosis

On the summer solstice, midsummer's day, they set off early to the Henge. They arrived about 11:30 am, which gave them time to rest before midday, when the sun is at its highest in the midsummer sky.

Matilda took off her backpack and took out a long white shift dress. She slipped off her t-shirt and jodis and put on the dress, she went barefoot.

She untacked Prince and took out a stable rubber to wipe his face and his back. Then, they went into the centre of the Henge. Prince stood in the exact centre of the circle.

As the sun climbed up to its highest point, a huge ray of light shone down onto him.

He reared up onto his hind legs and seemed to grow before Matilda's eyes.

As the magical ray of midsummer sun hit his feet, with a great flash, it cut his hooves into two toes, making them cloven hooves. They were silver!

The magical ray of light zapped all around his head and his horn began to grow, it was an awesome silver spiral!

The light sped from his horn, down his neck, along his back to his tail. His mane and tail were longer, they were sleeker and glistened silver in the magical ray of sunlight.

The magic ran all around him, all through him.

He reared up to his full height, shaking his silver mane.

Feeling the magic running through him, filled him with strength.

Suddenly, there was a magical flash of light and his wings were fully formed, they were silver and just awesome.

Prince reared up onto his hind legs again and called out, "Now I am a full unicorn."

It was a bit scary, but Matilda felt calm, because Prince had promised her she would be safe with him to protect her and she trusted him.

She took a deep breath and swallowed hard. As the sun passed over the sky, it left the Henge and the magical ray of light disappeared. Matilda rubbed her eyes to adjust them to the normal light and then, suddenly, she saw the changes in Prince.

He was about two hands taller, his mane and tail had grown and were shining silver. His horn had grown and was an amazing silver spiral.

His hooves were now cloven and were silver, but the most incredible magical happening of all, were his awesome silver wings!

It was just so exciting to think that soon they would be able to actually fly!

Wow, she thought, *he's going to be just like his sire, the King of all unicorns.*

All of this seemed to be over in seconds, but as Matilda was getting changed into her riding clothes, she glanced at her watch and noticed that two hours had passed.

When tacking up, Matilda took quite a long time to fit the saddle behind those amazing wings. Prince said that it felt strange wearing a saddle now that he had wings.

"When we get home, we'll put the saddle away. I'll ride bareback, if it's more comfortable for you, Prince," Matilda said.

"Yes, I would like that, my wings will keep you safe Matilda," said Prince.

She mounted up. Prince said, "Take a big handful of my mane, to be sure you feel secure. Sit tight – here we go Matilda!"

He opened his magnificent wings and with a huge leap, he took to the air and they were flying and as they circled over the stone circle, Matilda remembered the day that he was born. The day she first threw her arms around his neck and she closed her eyes. She had felt that they were flying. Now it was really happening and it was so exciting, she kept her eyes wide open!

"Oh Prince," she said, "I've dreamed of this day and what a day it has been! Now we're actually flying!"

Prince spiralled downwards, Matilda threw her arms up into the air and called out, "Wooo Hooo!"

We must remember that only Diva, Prince's dam, Matilda and those who live in the magical realm, can see Prince as a unicorn. To ordinary people, he is just a very handsome grey horse, but we know differently, don't we; and this is only the beginning of their adventures together.